DANGER! ACTION! TROUBLE! ADVENTURE!

THE D·A·T·A SET

A Little Snow Must Fall

HELLO!
HELLO!

By Ada Hopper
Illustrated by Rafael Kirschner of Glass House Graphics

LITTLE SIMON
New York   London   Toronto   Sydney   New Delhi

LITTLE SIMON
An imprint of Simon & Schuster Children's Publishing Division
1230 Avenue of the Americas, New York, New York 10020
First Little Simon paperback edition December 2023
Copyright © 2023 by Simon & Schuster, Inc.
Also available in a Little Simon hardcover edition

For information about special discounts for bulk purchases, please contact Simon & Schuster Special Sales at 1-866-506-1949 or business@simonandschuster.com.
The Simon & Schuster Speakers Bureau can bring authors to your live event. For more information or to book an event contact the Simon & Schuster Speakers Bureau at 1-866-248-3049 or visit our website at www.simonspeakers.com.
Designed by Joohn Kwon
Manufactured in the United States of America 1023 LAK
10 9 8 7 6 5 4 3 2 1
This book has been cataloged with the Library of Congress.
ISBN 978-1-6659-4914-9 (hc)
ISBN 978-1-6659-4913-2 (pbk)
ISBN 978-1-6659-4915-6 (ebook)

CONTENTS

Chapter 1

A Winter Thrill

"The current temperature is thirty degrees," Gabe said as he finished his calculations.

"Tir-ty!" squealed his little sister, Juanita.

"Wind is at perfect velocity," Gabe added.

"City! City!" repeated Juanita as

her winter hat slipped down over her face.

"Not city. Ve-lo-ci-ty." Gabe smiled and helped her lift her hat. "Velocity means the speed and direction of an object."

"Gabe, she's only two," Laura said. "Don't you think she's a little young for a physics lesson?"

"It's never too early to learn," Gabe declared.

Fluffy white snow blanketed all of Newtonburg. Gabe, Olive, Cesar, and Laura were enjoying a rare snow day in Gabe's backyard. The four whiz kids were eager to test Laura's new sled that she designed. They weren't known as the DATA Set for nothing, after all.

"Did your mom really let you babysit Juanita?" asked Olive.

"Nah," admitted Gabe. "She's watching by the window, but she thinks we can't see her."

"That tracks," said Cesar. "At least we get an extra cool test driver."

"Extra! Extra!" shouted Juanita.

"Okay, we are all set!" said Olive.

She proudly presented two snow mounds she had just finished building.

"This little one is the Cricket," Olive explained. "It's the perfect slope for Juanita, so she goes fast, but not too fast. And this slope is the Brain Scrambler. It's SUPER fast."

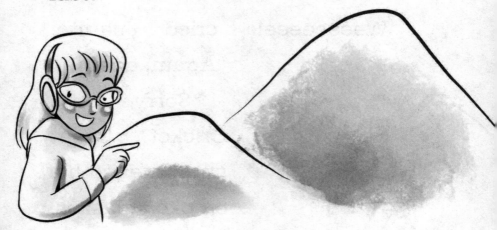

"Let's do this!" cheered the friends.

Juanita was up first. Gabe gave her a gentle push down the small hill.

"Weeeeeeee!" cried Juanita. "Again, again!"

"Sorry, little Cricket." Cesar straightened his crooked glasses.

"But it's time to get scrambled. And I'm not talking about eggs."

Cesar carried Laura's sled up to the very top of the Brain Scrambler. He took a deep breath and pushed off.

"SCRAMBLE!" he shouted.

The DATA Set's eyes grew wide as Cesar sailed through the air for a long time before crashing back down to the soft snow.

KA-BOOM!

"Oh no!" exclaimed Laura. "Did my sled explode—with Cesar ON it?!"

Olive and Laura hurried to check on their friend.

From underneath the snow,

POOF!

Cesar popped up with a huge grin. "That—was—EPIC!"

"What was that loud explosion?" asked Olive.

Cesar shrugged. "Wasn't me. My brain may be scrambled, but it didn't blow up. Oh, we should build a hill called the BRAIN EXPLODER!"

Gabe climbed to the top of the
the Brain Scrambler and pointed.
"I think I found our answer."

Chapter 2

Snowball 2

A small cloud of smoke hung over the teetering old Victorian house that loomed at the end of the street. It was the home of their slightly mad scientist friend, Dr. Gustav Bunsen.

After dropping Juanita off with Gabe's mom, the DATA Set rushed over to Bunsen's house and hurried to his secret laboratory.

"Dr. B., are you okay?" Laura called.

Dr. Bunsen popped out from behind an unusual-looking invention. It looked like a large metal ring with a picture of a

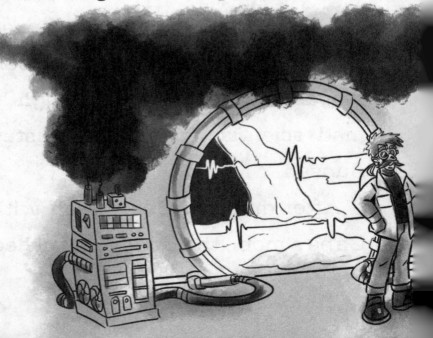

snowy cave scene inside. The doctor wore full winter gear. His hair was its usual messy orange mop.

"Ah! Just the fearless foursome I was hoping to see!" he exclaimed.

"We heard an explosion," Laura said. "Is everything okay?"

"Oh yes, quite all right," the doctor assured them. Though the DATA Set knew that Dr. B. had a different definition of "all right" than most scientists. A T. rex could be thundering toward him and Bunsen would joyfully count its teeth.

"Did the boom come from this thing?" Olive asked.

The DATA Set gathered around it curiously.

"Indeed! It was just a slight malfunction with my Habitat Breakaway 4000." Bunsen pointed to his invention. "Behold! A door to different environments all over the world!"

The friends watched in amazement as the winter scene inside the ring switched to an image of a desert, then a rain forest.

"Cool!" Cesar said. "I bet you could see all kinds of animals

through this . . . uh . . . spying thing?"

"It looks more like a portal," Gabe said.

"You're both correct," said the doctor. "I've been sending my Bunsen Buddy Bots to study animals all over the world. But one of them just came back with a very strange message."

Suddenly, a robot penguin waddled out from behind the doctor. It was just a little taller than a regular penguin, with a metal body and blinking laser-red eyes. It also had a small screen that flashed messages across its tummy.

HELLO! HELLO! it read.

"Awwww!" cooed Laura.

"Meet Snowball 2," Dr. Bunsen said proudly. "My Antarctic explorer. Each Bunsen Buddy Bot is designed to blend in with the local creatures."

Snowball 2 waved hello with its metal flipper. Its tummy message changed from HELLO! TO HELP! HELP! HELP!

"That doesn't look good," Laura

said. "Does it need an oil change?"

"Actually, that's the strange message I was talking about," Dr. Bunsen admitted. "Snowball 2 has been flashing it ever since returning from Antarctica. But I'm not quite sure why."

Gabe leaned down to inspect the robot more closely. "Can't you just ask?"

Dr. B shook his head. "It has limited language function so it can blend better in with the real penguins. At least, better than . . . the one before."

"The one before?" Olive asked.

"Oh, nothing!" The doctor quickly looked away. "Anyways, I'll have to upload Snowball 2's data to my computer to understand what it needs. It may take a few hours."

"We can help," Gabe offered.

The penguin flashed an angry face on its tummy. No Time.

Suddenly, Snowball 2 reached out a mechanical flipper and zapped the Habitat Breakaway. It was now a scene of an icy cave. Without warning, Snowball 2 hugged Gabe and hopped into the portal. A second later, the winter scene changed to a tropical beach.

The DATA Set gasped. Gabe and Snowball 2 were gone!

Chapter 3

March of the DATA Set!

"No way!" exclaimed Cesar, pulling at his hair. "Gabe's been penguin-napped!"

"Dr. B., we have to go after him!" cried Laura.

"Right!" exclaimed the doctor. He picked up a controller and gave the Habitat Breakaway 4000 a good zap. The invention flipped through a few scenes before landing on a quiet, snowy landscape.

"That doesn't look like the same snow cave from earlier," Olive said.

"Are you sure?" the doctor asked. "Surely it can't be too far off."

"Isn't Antarctica more than five million square miles?" Cesar asked. "I remember that from my book report."

"Indeed," Dr. B. said brightly. "We'd better hurry along."

Luckily, the Data Set was already dressed for the journey. Snug in

their winter gear, they took a step forward.

"One step for the DATA Set. One giant leap across the world!" Dr. B said. "Now, focus very clearly on stepping through the portal. All together now, quickly!"

The kids took a deep breath. "One . . . two . . . three . . . JUMP!"

They hopped into the wintry
scene but didn't arrive there in
a single leap. Instead, they fell
through a dizzying tunnel of
flashing colors and lights.

"My brain is getting scrambled
again!" Cesar cried.

Almost as soon as it had started, the spinning stopped. They landed in a heap of fluffy snow.

"Now that's what I want my sled to feel like!" Laura exclaimed. She scooped out the snow that had gathered in her hood.

Next to her, Olive shivered. "It's so c-c-c-cold. I don't think

our snowsuits are meant for Antarctica."

Cesar popped out of a snow mound. "It's like living in an ice cream f-f-f-freezer!"

"Never fear!" Dr. Bunsen reached into his pocket and revealed four snowflake-shaped pins. "Put these on your coats and you'll feel as toasty as, well, toast."

With shaking hands, they clipped the pins to their jackets. Instantly, a pleasant warmth spread throughout their snowsuits. It was like wearing their own personal heaters.

"That's better," Olive sighed, feeling cozier. "But what about Gabe? I don't see him anywhere."

"And I don't see footprints," Laura observed.

But Dr. B. didn't look worried. "Snowball 2 is equipped with a spare snowflake pin," Dr. B said. "I

am perfectly sure Gabe is in great hands. I mean, flippers."

Determined, Dr. Bunsen pulled out his controller and adjusted a few knobs. It began beeping loudly.

"Huzzah!" the doctor exclaimed. "The Bunsen Buddy Bot tracker has picked up their signal."

"Is it . . . ," Cesar gulped, thinking of the continent's giant size, ". . . five million miles away?"

"Only half a mile!" cheered the doctor. "This way!"

The friends squinted out over the blinding white landscape. A flock of penguins marched single file over a frozen hill.

"Penguins!" Olive exclaimed. "Maybe Snowball 2 took Gabe to where the penguins are going."

"Fantastic observation, Olive!" cried the doctor. "Explorers— march on!"

Chapter 4

Follow That Penguin

Head still spinning from the portal, Gabe sat up slowly.

"Ugh . . . where am I?" he muttered. It was dark all around him . . . except for a red laser shining in his face.

"Whoa!" Gabe jumped back, bumping into a snowy wall.

The red light blinked, then backed away. Gabe breathed a sigh of relief. It was just Snowball 2's laser eye. The penguin had extended it to study Gabe where he sat.

They were inside an icy cave.

Gabe hugged himself. "It's freezing in here! How are you

able to function at such a low temperature?"

Then he realized he wasn't actually that cold at all. "Okay, now I'm freaking out. Why am I so warm?"

A mechanical clicking echoed in the cave as Snowball 2 approached Gabe. With a flipper, it tapped on something attached to the front of Gabe's coat. There was a snowflake-shaped pin Gabe had never seen before.

Pin. Pin. Pin. The words flashed across Snowball 2's belly. Warm. Warm. Warm.

Gabe frowned. "You mean, this tiny pin is keeping me warm? Whoa! Sounds like one of Dr. B's genius inventions." He stood and

looked around at the emptiness of the cave. "But how come you brought me through the portal?"

A familiar message flashed across Snowball 2's belly in the dark. HELP! HELP! HELP!

"How?" Gabe asked. "In case you haven't noticed, I'm not from Antarctica. I don't even know if I've ever tried speaking to a penguin before."

Snowball 2 didn't answer. Instead, it began to waddle deeper into the cave. Gabe followed close by, surprised at how beautiful the snowy cave turned out to be.

They passed by rooms made of ice with icicles forming

decorations on the walls. Tiny, frozen snowflakes hovered in the air. It was the closest thing to a winter wonderland that Gabe had ever seen. It was like art.

"Whoa," Gabe marveled. "You can't find this in Newtonburg, that's for sure. Snowball 2, is this what you need help with? Making . . . ice art?"

The penguin only sped up its pace down the long tunnel. Before long, they reached a fork in their path.

"Which way?" Gabe asked. "Left? Or right?"

Instead of turning any which way, Snowball 2's flipper feet suddenly retracted inside its body. Two penguin-sized skis popped

out in their place. The screen on its belly became a large flashlight.

Snowball 2 leaned its body forward and slid down the icy tunnel on the right.

"Wait!" Gabe cried. "You're taking all the light with you!"

Gabe followed the Bunsen Buddy Bot deeper into the cave.

Chapter 5

Arctic Attack!

"Look at them," Olive marveled. "There are so many!"

The DATA Set crouched behind a snowdrift, observing the huge crowd of penguins. The birds squawked and waddled. It was a giant penguin party!

"Those are emperor penguins,"

Cesar explained. "This must be their nesting site." He pointed to a group of smaller, soft-gray penguins. "Oh, and those are the babies!"

"This is all really cute, but I still don't see Gabe," said Laura. "Or Snowball 2."

Doctor Bunsen flicked his controller. "These readings are very odd. See how the tracker keeps disappearing? Wait—it's coming closer now!"

Olive looked over Dr. B.'s shoulder and frowned. "Uh—isn't it coming in fast?"

The friends watched the blinking red light approach faster than any penguin could waddle.

"I don't think that's Snowball 2 . . . ," Cesar said slowly.

The team looked up. The beeping became faster just as a huge creature with massive paws appeared on the hilltop!

Laura gasped. "Is that . . . a polar bear? In Antarctica?!"

"It can't be," Olive said. "Polar bears live up north in the Arctic. Not Antarctica."

Squawk! Squawk! Squawk!

The penguins rushed around in alarm as the polar bear thundered forward.

"It's going to crash into them!" cried Olive.

But to their surprise, the giant creature wasn't heading for the penguins. It was heading straight for the DATA Set!

"RUN!" cried Cesar.

Cesar, Laura, and Olive scrambled to their feet, slipping in the snow. But Bunsen ran straight toward the bear!

"Dr. B., wait!" shouted Cesar. "You'll get polar pounced!"

The doctor and the bear both skidded to a sudden stop, staring into each other's eyes.

"He's a goner!" moaned Olive.

Then something odd happened. The polar bear nuzzled Dr. B.! Dr. B laughed and nuzzled it back.

"Whaaaaa—?" The friends carefully made their way over.

"Could someone please explain what's going on?" Laura asked.

The doctor joyfully scratched behind the bear's ears. "DATA Set, meet Snowball 1!"

"Snowball 1?" they repeated.

Suddenly, the bear blinked

and had laser eyes, just like Snowball 2.

"But why is Snowball 1 a polar bear?" Laura asked, confused. "Aren't your Bunsen Buddy Bots supposed to blend in?"

"Ah, well, a slight mix-up was bound to happen." Bunsen shrugged. "I have so many Bunsen Bots out and about. And you know how it is. Arctic. Antarctic. North. South. After a while, it all seems the same."

"Ooooookay . . . ," said Cesar.

"I tried to bring it home," Dr.

Bunsen continued. "But Snowball 1's beacon stopped responding. So I sent Snowball 2 in to find it." The doctor fiddled with a panel on the polar bear's back. "Aha! Just as I suspected. A piece of ice is lodged in the controls. This should do it!"

The doctor pulled a sharp icicle from the panel on Snowball 1's back. Instantly, its tracking signal beeped loud and clear.

Squawk! Squawk! The penguins angrily flapped their wings at the noise.

"You haven't seen Snowball 2, have you?" Laura asked the bear. "Or maybe our friend Gabe?"

"He's just about my height, dark hair, super smart?" Cesar added.

As if in response, Snowball 1 began plodding away in the snow.

"It looks like Snowball 1 knows the answer," Dr. Bunsen said. "Follow that adorable bear!"

Chapter 6

Penguin Peril

Gabe shielded his eyes as white light shone ahead. He had been following Snowball 2 through the cave tunnels for what seemed like forever.

"Oh good," he said in relief as his eyes adjusted to the light. "It's the entrance. If we get out, maybe

we can figure out a way to call for help."

Gabe took a step—and suddenly realized there was no snow beneath his foot!

"Whoa!" he shouted.

Snowball 2's flippers reached out and pulled him back.

"Thanks, buddy," Gabe said, then looked down. Between him and the cave entrance was a giant trench in the snow. It looked like a valley between two steep slopes.

"It's a good thing we didn't slip in," Gabe said. "I wouldn't be able to climb back out. How do we get across?"

But Snowball 2 only flashed its help signal once again. That's when Gabe heard faint squawks coming from below. Carefully, he looked over the edge of the ditch . . . and saw eight baby penguins trapped at the bottom!

"Oh no!" he exclaimed. "They're stuck! That must be why you needed us!" Gabe said. "How did they even get there?"

Snowball 2 flashed a new message across its belly. ROAR. ROAR. ROAR.

"You . . . want me to roar?"

Gabe asked. "Won't that just scare them? Um . . . okay." Standing tall, Gabe roared as loudly as he could.

Down below, the penguins all squawked in surprise. Then an unsettling cracking noise echoed in the cavern.

TROUBLE! TROUBLE! flashed the penguin's belly.

Snowball 2 zipped behind Gabe, extended its flippers to wrap them around Gabe, and then pushed off. Together, they slid down the slope right toward the baby penguins.

CRASH! A giant icicle fell from the cave ceiling right where they'd been standing!

"Ahhhhhhhh!" Gabe cried as he slid all the way to the bottom of

the trench. He landed right in the middle of the baby penguins. They scattered in surprise.

"That . . . was . . . close," Gabe breathed, looking up at the icicle that had fallen. "Thanks, buddy."

The robot penguin wobbled. WELCOME. WELCOME. WE-WE-WELCOME.

Gabe got to his feet. "Oh no. Snowball 2, are you . . . too cold to function?"

The robot's screen glitched for a moment. The robot shook its head, as if trying to focus.

Gabe studied the baby penguins. "Well . . . you can't really climb. You can't fly. And the only way out is . . . well, way up there."

The baby penguins looked at one another doubtfully. Gabe didn't blame them. It was going to take a lot of physics to solve this one.

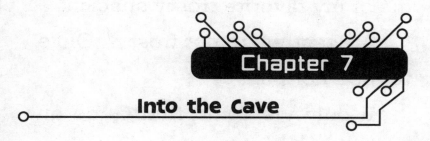

Chapter 7

Into the Cave

"Snow cones. Ice cream. Frosted cereal," Cesar mumbled as the DATA Set and Dr. Bunsen followed Snowball 1 through the snow. "Cesar, why are you talking about food?" Olive laughed.

"I'm hungry." Cesar hugged his belly. "I only had breakfast and then the first snack after breakfast. And this snow keeps reminding me of my favorite frosty snacks."

"At least we're not frosty." Olive tapped her pin.

"If only we could find Gabe on your tracker, Dr. B.," Cesar groaned. "I can't walk five million miles."

Just then, Snowball 1 grunted in the direction of a massive ice chunk. The polar bear lifted a giant paw and urged them to follow.

"You know, ice is kind of beautiful," Laura said. "The whole place is basically covered in sculptures of ice."

"I think that's the iceberg the Titanic hit in 1912," Cesar joked.

"That's no iceberg." Olive's eyes grew wide. "It's a cave! Dr. B. . . . if Gabe and Snowball 2 are in there, would the ice block the robot's tracker?"

"It certainly might," the doctor agreed. "There's only one way to find out."

With a fresh spurt of energy, the group hurried to the cave entrance.

"Hello in there!" Cesar cupped his hands around his mouth like a megaphone. "Any Snowballs home? Preferably Snowball 2 and Snowball Gabe?"

"Cesar? Is that you?" a voice echoed from inside in the cavern.

That voice was very familiar! The friends sprinted forward. But

suddenly, Snowball 1 leaped in front and blocked their path.

"Hey, what are you—whoa!" Laura cried.

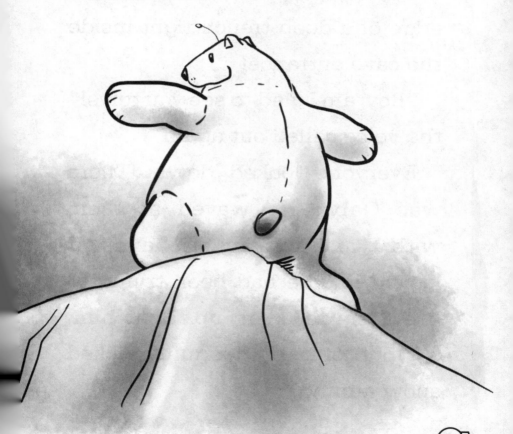

They had almost fallen over the edge of a deep trench right inside the cave entrance!

"Boy, am I glad to see you guys!" the voice called out again.

Everyone looked down. There was Gabe! He waved at them with two icicles in his hands. It looked like he had been trying to use them to climb up. Near him, a group of baby penguins kicked snow around.

"Well, you're stuck in a pickle!"
Dr. B called out. "Or a ditch."

"I'm fine!" Gabe shouted. "But
we can't get out, and Snowball 2
is glitching."

HELLO. HELLO. Snowball 2 flashed. WELCOME. WELCOME. HELP. HELP. ROAR. ROAR.

"Those are a whole lot of words that don't go together," Cesar said.

But Dr. Bunsen smacked his head. "Of course! I programmed Snowball 1 with the typical roar of a polar bear. It must have accidentally scared the young penguins into this cave and into an

icy trap. Now we're all here, too!"

"*ROAR!*" Snowball 1 growled, proving Dr. Bunsen's point.

At that moment, a terrible cracking noise echoed through the cavern.

Chapter 8

Slippery Slope

A crooked crack formed at the top of the cave, then quickly raced down toward the group.

FWOOMP! Snowball 1 shoved Olive, Laura, Cesar, and Dr. Bunsen out of the way just in time.

CRASH! Icicles fell where they had been standing.

"Oh yeah," Gabe said. "I forgot to mention the falling icicles . . ."

"Yikes!" exclaimed Cesar. "We were almost turned into shaved ice!"

Danger. Danger. Snowball 2's belly screen flashed. It pointed up at the remaining icicles with a frantic flipper.

The cave's ceiling was covered with large, pointy icicles that could break free at any moment.

"Can we use the Habitat thing-a-majig to beam Gabe and the penguins out?" Cesar asked.

Too Loud. Too Loud. Snowball 2's
screen flashed.

"I think loud noises are what
cause the icicles to fall," Gabe
explained.

"And the Habitat Breakaway
isn't the quietest invention." Olive
remembered the explosion from
Dr. Bunsen's house.

"What if we used it outside the cave to go back to his lab and get an invention to help rescue them?" Laura suggested.

No Time. No Time. Snowball 2 flashed.

A slight shudder rumbled through the cave, and the icicles vibrated. The baby penguins squawked nervously and huddled around Gabe.

"Do you have a rope?" Laura asked Dr. B. hopefully.

The doctor patted his pockets, then sighed. "Alas, it's in my other parka."

Cesar tapped his chin in thought. Then he remembered how Snowball 2 had extended its flippers in the lab. The penguin was glitching, but they still had the polar bear.

"Maybe Snowball 1 could lower us down," Cesar suggested. "Like a human rope."

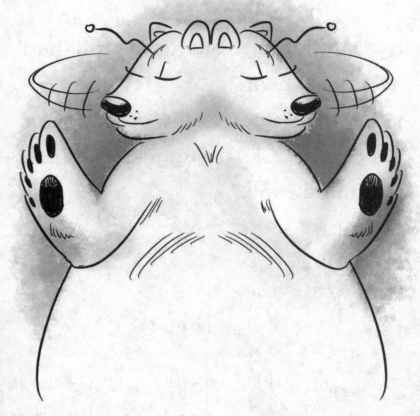

But the polar shook its head and lifted its paws.

"They don't extend like the flippers," Dr. B said.

"Well, now I'm really wishing we'd brought your sled, Laura," Olive sighed. "With this slope, imagine how quickly we'd be able to move."

"It would be fast. . . ." Laura's voice trailed off. Her gaze fell on a slightly flatter part of the slope near the bottom of the opposite trench wall.

"Dr. B., how much does Snowball 1 weigh?" she asked.

"About two hundred kilograms," the doctor said.

Olive followed Laura's gaze. "Oh! Its weight plus ours, and the right trajectory and angle . . ."

"Are you thinking what I'm thinking?" Laura asked.

"It should work." Olive nodded.

"But we'd only have one chance to get it right."

"With Snowball 1's help, we could do it." Laura's eyes shone bright.

"Okay, I'm lost," Cesar said. "What are you two talking about?"

Olive and Laura shared a grin. "It's time to go sledding!"

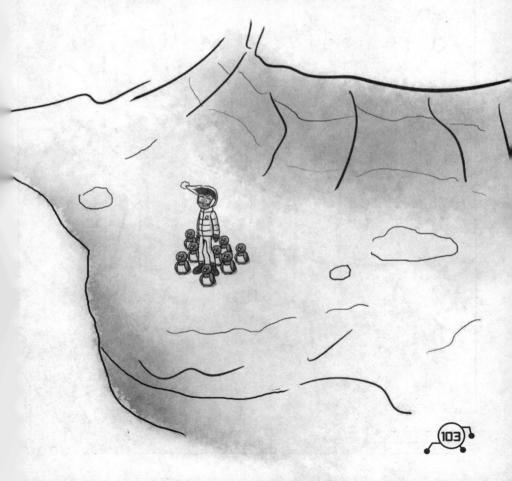

Chapter 9

Habitat Breakaway

"Sledding?" Cesar asked. "Do you guys have brain freeze? If we go down, then we'll all be trapped!"

"Trust us!" Laura exclaimed. "It will only work if we all do it. We need everyone's weight."

She quickly explained the plan. With a fallen icicle, in the soft snow

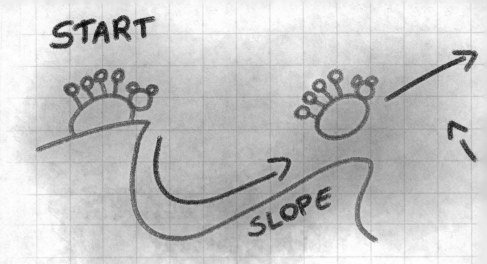

she drew the slope of the cliff they stood on. "If Gabe can build up enough snow down there, it will be like the ramp I made in Gabe's backyard. And we'll use Snowball 1 as the sled."

"All we need to do is hop onto Snowball 1's back and ride down," Olive continued.

She drew a line to show how they would swoop down and then out of the trench. "Snowball 1's robot weight, plus ours, will give us enough velocity to sail up and over the trench edge."

"How do I join the fun?" Gabe asked from down below.

"As we reach the bottom of the trench, Snowball 2 can use one flipper to latch onto you and one to grab onto us. That way, you'll fly free!" Laura finished.

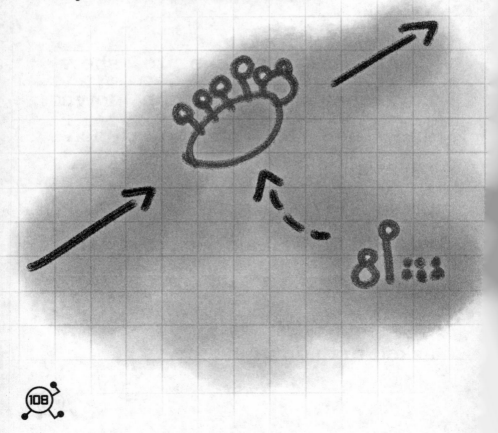

"Though, don't forget to bring the baby penguins along with you," Olive said. "A big warm hug should help."

"Genius!" Bunsen cheered.

A rumble shuddered the cave again and the icicles trembled.

"It's the only way," Olive insisted. "Let's go! Did you get all of that, Gabe?"

"Loud and clear!" Gabe replied. "Snowball 2, can you do it?"

Still slightly glitchy, Snowball 2 nodded. It extended its flippers once, twice, and then squawked instructions at the baby penguins. Luckily, they listened happily.

Gabe got to work immediately. He and Snowball 2 began piling up enough snow to slide up and out of the trench. When it was done, he gave his friends a thumbs-up.

"Ready?" Laura asked.

"As ready as I'll ever be." Cesar gulped.

"Onward!" Bunsen said.

"Three, two, one, go!" said Laura.

Chapter 10

Home Sweet Home

The icy wind whipped past the friends as they zoomed down the ramp.

"I'm gonna lose my breakfast...." Cesar gritted his teeth. Clutching Snowball 1's back, the team was nearly at the bottom.

Snowball 2 used one extended

flipper to grab Gabe, while Gabe held all the baby penguins in a big hug.

"Steady . . . steady . . . ." Gabe watched the polar bear come closer. "Are you ready,

Snowball 2? And . . . get set . . . GO!"

Just as Snowball 1 passed them, the robot penguin latched onto Dr. Bunsen. The doctor held on as the group was pulled into the air.

"WOOOO!" Gabe cheered.

FWOOMP! Snowball 1 landed safely on the other side of the trench, sliding on its belly.

They did it!

And not a moment too soon. The cave shuddered the moment they all landed.

"Run for it!" Gabe shouted.

Everyone sprinted out of the cave just as icicles dropped down from the ceiling, smashing to the bottom of the trench!

"Phew!" Cesar's voice was shaky. "I know the D in DATA Set stands for 'Danger,' but can we please stop cutting it so close?"

"Is everyone all right?" Doctor Bunsen asked.

Squawk, squawk, squawk! The baby penguins nuzzled Snowball 2.

"We are now," Gabe said gratefully. "And I think I know just how the baby penguins are feeling. I'm so glad you all came!"

"We couldn't let you have all the fun," Laura joked.

Squawk! Squawk! The DATA Set watched as adult penguins hurried over from a snow hill, calling out to their babies.

"I wish we could stay longer and play with them," Olive said.

"Me too," said Cesar. "But we should get home. It's definitely time for lunch."

"We can visit one day," Dr. Bunsen assured them. "Thanks to

science, we're but a zap away."

With a click of his controller, he opened a portal back to his laboratory. They waved to the penguins and the Bunsen Bot Buddies before stepping through.

As soon as they were in Dr. B's

lab, Cesar flopped onto the floor. "I've never been so happy to see Newtonburg before."

"What will happen to Snowball 1?" Laura asked Dr. Bunsen. "Will you send him to the Arctic instead?"

"Most likely," the doctor replied. "Unless he prefers somewhere warmer."

"So if we see a polar bear in Australia on the news," Olive giggled, "we'll know where he came from."

Back at home, the DATA Set found Gabe's mom waiting for them in the kitchen.

"Why do you all look so tired?" she asked. "Long snow day?"

"Snow! Snow!" Juanita cried out. She sat on the ground, scooping ice cream from a small bowl. Her face was covered in chocolate.

"You could say that." Laura laughed.

Gabe's mom smiled. "Sounds like ice cream sandwiches are well-deserved."

"All right!" Cesar fist-pumped. "Now that's a frosty treat I'd walk five million miles for."

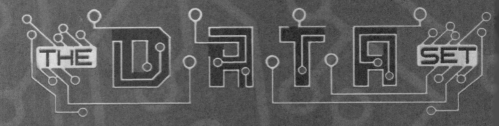

THE D·A·T·A SET

FOR MORE DANGER! ACTION! TROUBLE! ADVENTURE!

Check out all the previous books!